The Burial

Georg

Mike de Sousa

The Burial of Georgio Sánchez

Mike de Sousa

All rights reserved. No part of this book may be reproduced in any form or by any electronic or mechanical means, including information storage and retrieval systems, without written permission from the author, except in the case of a reviewer, who may quote brief passages embodied in critical articles or in a review.

This is a work of fiction. Names, characters, places, and incidents are the product of the author's imagination. Any resemblance to actual persons, living or dead, events, or locales, is entirely coincidental.

All Rights Reserved: Mike de Sousa © 2012

Published by: EyeInvent Publishing

www.EyeInventPublishing.com

February 2012

Copyright © 2012 Mike de Sousa

www.mikedesousa.com

All rights reserved.

ISBN-10: 1469940671
ISBN-13: 978-1469940670

SUMMARY

The Burial of Georgio Sánchez draws the reader into a world of complex relationships and divided loyalties within a small community, as the accidental death of Georgio Sánchez leads to the substitution of his body for that of the only witness to an earlier killing.

Protagonists commit crimes of conscience in a deceptively short work that unfurls rich layers, and rewards the diligent reader at each turn. The chronologies of events, combined with the characters' recollections of past incidents, create an evocation of their passions, self-sacrifice, and necessary deceit.

The narrative is presented in the second person, and the story unfolds from a variety of viewpoints. Changes in perspective are denoted by a central bullet point:

•

REACTIONS TO THE BURIAL OF GEORGIO SÁNCHEZ

"Wonderfully written and beautifully poetic…" Bloomsbury

"Highly individual and imaginative…" Michael Berkeley

"Written with sensitivity and delicacy…" Flambard Press

"Full of marvellous things…" Martin Secker and Warburg

"Bold and innovative…" Picador

Mike de Sousa

CONTENTS

	Passwords	i
1	A Dust Filled Land	1
2	Within The Wing Beat of a Hummingbird	5
3	The Blaze of Headlight, The Closing Space	19
4	The Full-Throated Sound of Impact	29
5	He is Still Warm, Feel Him	33
6	The Severed Finger	39
7	The Heat of Secrecy Burns Between You	51
8	The Half-Light	59
9	Desire and Deceit	69
10	When Alone Two Things Remain	77

PASSWORDS

• • •

To tell the truth,

The boundary blurs between now,

And then.

Between one point of view,

•

And another.

Between what is spoken,

And what is written.

1. A DUST FILLED LAND

• • •

The bus bumps and brakes, sounds babble in uncomfortable unison as the woman views the tattered piece of paper she folds, then unfolds.

. . . When alone two things remain . . .

She folds, her eyes unsighted she unfolds.

You have been watching her for the last hour, every now and then she repeats a phrase to herself then crimps the note once more. You have spent this time deciphering the words that fleetingly pass her lips and have come to know the words but not the language. You strike many thoughts to stone. You have noticed how sadness bathes her beauty . . . If the old man snoring by your side woke, you would cross the centre aisle and speak with her. With jolts and starts he snorts immersed in dream, sporadic flicking of his arms and legs belch unconscious from his world to yours. He is too large to climb over without waking.

●

You fold, you unfold,

You look upon the bottle held in your hand half full with ink, then, not an inch beyond, the mingling of its shadow and light jewelled against the pale sand-softened windowed wall. You think of your mother, confused contesting thoughts.

Why your mother at this time?

It is something that was sensed, the quality of light that reminds you, her necklace of finely sculpted glass, sharpened points of lustre prickling the cold air, mesmeric, both a feeling of discomfort and enjoyment will your fragile sight, as headlamps in the darkness to a child.

Between the intermittent scenes of ever changing forms, the rambling tone of wireless, peasant faces scorched indelibly in your mind, the bus bumps and brakes across a dust filled land towards what seems as ember to the west, the shimmering trace of skyline.

●

You are not so much asleep as the young man seated by your side believes.

You too have been watching.

You are old, although younger than a first impression might imply. Since the day your only love left your body has endured complete neglect. You spend your days feigning sleep on the public transport that travels from one town to the next, it is the only method you have found where by you may enter into the intimate world of others. You feel starved of significant contact, for whenever you begin a conversation with a stranger you are met with indifference. You have passed the point of despair and having found your need of friendship still so cruelly obstructed, you have adopted a strategy that may seem more passive than active.

You glance again at the young man with powder blue eyes. You jolt the narrative, frustrate the reader, for in your quietened world of unmoving, protagonists may not meet. Reprisal for the embitterment of loneliness. You, the old man who is younger than a first impression might imply, grunt with the inward satisfaction of delightful deceit.

●

Foot flush to the deck you rush swerving the bus this way then that, not because the pretty young woman with impassioned eyes implored you to reach the small town by daybreak, but to spend the early hours by Aura's side ahead of her husband's return.

You notice the old man in your mirror, you have driven him to and fro on this route on many occasions. You do not understand how he sleeps throughout the sight of such a beautiful land.

You look at the road lit by two beams of tungsten light. You fail to remember driving over an inch of the last treacherous mile of dust and stone. Shrugging your shoulders you think again of the warm welcome that awaits.

●

You fold you unfold you whisper

When alone two things remain.

All occur within the space of a breath.

You look:

Words collapse as the image of a small town comes to view, printed by your father on the belly of a tattered piece of paper you fold then unfold.

2. WITHIN THE WING BEAT OF A HUMMINGBIRD

• • •

Pinpricks of starlight come teeming over the roofs and walls of Pueblo del Pocito to greet the gaze of José Cabrera. He has been woken by the muffled murmur of another's dream and is now sitting at his desk. An oil lamp hangs from the unlit ceiling as he watches Aura gently kiss the door to doorframe then step out into the chill night air. She moves with unpretentious pride and dignity, her manner is neither hesitant nor suspicious as she walks to the church of San Juan Bautista. José trims the wick, pulls a box of matches from his trouser pocket then lights the lamp. Sulphur drifts as gradually the spit of sparks subside. He settles, lifts a piece of paper from the pile, then begins to draw the acanthus leaves that cover the broken-edged arch of the church doorway. It is not unusual for José to work long into the night so Aura is not surprised when the glow of lamplight crosses the street from his home to meet her. She passes the atrium in front of the church, pauses then listens:

That sound, Guillermo's bus?

You raise your head,

One thirty, too soon,

You continue,

It is late . . . He will understand the intrusion.

You knock.

Luis Martinez had been appointed acting parish priest seven months previously, it is his first position of responsibility.

Your husband?

No, not yet. . .

Quickly, close the door.

Incense clings to the air as Father Luis Martinez and Aura Delgardo speak. Voices ricochet then return in broken unfamiliar whispers by the shadows of saints that crowd the muraled canopy of the church interior. Below, votive candles flicker, naked to the breath of their confession.

Guillermo, you expect Guillermo tonight?

Yes.

We must act swiftly, you say Felipe has not returned?

No, he is due to carry out his duties until first light, he will be back an hour later.

Were you seen?

No. . . Wait, José, his light was on.

José Cabrera?

Yes.

He is a good man.

The face of his Bible acts as Braille to the palm.

It will not matter, I am sure of it.

Aura sifts the contents of the inner pocket to her tunic; a handkerchief, two coins of little value, her permit, the pouch:

You hug the soft warmth of velvet between your fingers hearing the stifled sound of delicate glass to glass. You sense its weight, perfect in your hand.

Here, Felipe hid it from me a few days before Father Antonio's disappearance.

The priest places his Bible on the pew, takes the pouch then loosens the ribbon that runs through its hem spilling the glass necklace out onto his hand.

You are sure?

Aura closes her eyes then gently tilts her head.

I know my husband, he plans to use it against Guillermo. He'll say he stole it. He can only try the once, you should have it until then. . . take it. . . . Luis?

. . . We must not say a word, if you are right Felipe will act soon, in the meantime I shall find a place for this.

Talk to my sister Leticia, I came from there tonight, she does not believe Felipe would harm anyone, she will listen to you.

●

With the shutters closed the baked brick floor will stay warm for the rest of night. You may need the single blanket that lays folded length-ways beneath you. Your eyes open, it is twenty minutes since Aura left for the church.

Your head fills with the sporadic recollection of past incident:

I've had the blanket double woven for you.

Thank you José, it is more than I could have hoped for.

I'm glad you like it.

Father, don't you think. . .

Leticia is right José, beautiful work, now, will you consider my proposal, the frontispiece for the new Bibles? . . I know, I know but before you utter a word at least say you'll think about it. Listen, you need the money, the church is rich, the people poor. Some disposal of parish funds would profit us all. Bring over the pencil sketches you made a week ago eh?

Father Antonio pats his watch then places a hand on José's shoulder.

I'll see you tonight, we'll talk then.

José smiles then nods.

You shiver then turn onto your side. You unfold the diamond-centred blanket that compels connection with another place:

You cover yourself. Your eyes remain open. A rap at the door, you are startled.

Felipe.

May I come in?

Of course, sit down, you are shaking, take this.

He covers himself with your blanket with the words

You've seen Aura?

Earlier.

She is unhurt?

Yes.

And Father Antonio?

He is with José.

You push a splint of wood firmly into the belly of the iron stove then half fill the kettle with water.

Coffee?

You are not worried?

Trust me, they are safe.

I . . .

Even at this time of evident strain Felipe's voice holds the strength of tone that gained him his position as counsellor to the district courts. His task is to advise on difficult cases, ones in which the law's ambiguous prose gives no direct guidance as to the guilt or sentence of the defendant.

. . . I was called upon today to act as advocate for an elderly woman who, while admitting the crime of murder, remains inconsolable at the death of her son.

You feel these words fall like the gentle puff of rain on the dusty earth. Felipe has previously kept all mention of his work separate from your frequent contact, whether for protection you could not tell.

You listen with unexposed impatience.

•

Her name is Rosa.

You pause.

It is not that this pause is unduly long, that is to say longer than perhaps the time it takes for the warmth to escape from the cup you now hold. More that within this pause the nature of time shifts. An instant:

She listens with unexposed impatience.

Her name is Rosa.

Small amounts of breath expire with the fading sound of your voice.

The aroma of freshly pressed coffee beans fills the air. Vapour rises from the cup, sweating the left side of your forefinger that rests upon its rim. Blanket fibres flatten beneath the heat of its base.

You sense the slight pinch of shoelace tied too tightly. You clench your toes.

You hear the sizzle of dew escape the splint of wood Leticia fed to the stove not a minute before.

In your mind's eye you see Rosa in tears at the foot of her son's bed. Father Antonio stands silent at her side. To the left of him is a framed photograph of a young man seated by the open door of a large barn. He is smiling. You cannot see what is inside the barn as light from the next room catches the glass in front of the photograph.

You release your toes, sliding them smoothly along the shoe's leather lining. Lifting your heel you spread them full then draw a breath. The scent of coffee still pervades as Leticia speaks, her palm pressing down upon the lid squeezing an ounce of air from the tin.

There, you see? Father Antonio.

She calls you to the window. Father is still trying to convince José that he should work on the frontispiece for the new Bibles. Leticia turns, softening her voice.

They are safe in one another's company. Aura can take good care of herself.

You offer the blanket back with thanks.

Reprisals, I worry, my work, you understand.

Lowering the veil of distraction:

You mentioned, an old woman, you say she killed her son?

… Out of love.

Close to the fibre's edge

Rosa lived the years up until her thirty eighth birthday in a town two hundred miles to the north.

Her earliest memory

was of peering through a piece of white lace into a room covered with the fragments of woven fabric. The lace would tickle her nose as her eyes traced the passing patterns of the cloth. Fresh wood-shavings lay scattered under the warmth of the window, their fragrance lapping close to the fibre's edge.

Her father's forearms flexed as he fastened the bell above the door then climbed down the ladder, leaning it up against the small box-like shelves that spread the length and breadth of the facing wall. Her mother knelt sorting table linen, altar cloths, bedspreads, silk from flax, as the sound of ringing filled the store for the first time.

Rosa's father was a man who saw the world in certain terms, a thing was either beautiful or ugly, pleasing or repugnant, right or wrong. He would commit himself wholly to an action or not at all. It was this that brought him from Ireland to the New World, this that drove his ambition to found a career in the textile trade, and this that led him to marry into the purest blood of this land.

Felipe turns these words over in his mind as you might a brightly coloured marble in your hand, cold to the touch, foreign in its completeness. Suspended at its centre; bubbles of air, frozen as truth in honesty. He takes a sip from the cup swilling the thickening taste round his mouth then swallows

The world in certain terms:

C o m p l e t e   h u s h

Rosa spent the mornings up until her twelfth year in a single roomed school house seven minutes walk from her father's store.

Her last lesson

was to gather wild flowers that lay by the side of the path and take them in for study. Sun shone through the translucent pigment of green stems as Rosa cradled the freshly scented bundle in her left arm. Happily she brushed the dust that had collected on her dress and rushed into the classroom.

Complete hush.

●

You proudly walk to the front of the room and place the flowers on your teacher's folding wooden desk.

You notice your father standing close to the side door.

You smile.

Your father and teacher look directly into your eyes, a look of helpless confusion.

No one else ventures their glimpse towards you.

You look at the flowers once more.

Your father raises his arm,

You run to him.

Picking you up he holds you,

Too tightly,

You are shaking,

Both of you,

As one.

A fragment of gold leaf

Rosa's hair will touch the side of her waist as she turns to see who enters under the quickening to and fro of the bells fading.

She finds her father tugging at a thick newspaper that has been folded twice and forced two thirds through the shop-front letter-box. He has not yet felt your eyes rest on his struggling form. He straightens himself up, kicks the door and, cussing a few unfamiliar words, prepares for the next onslaught. Rosa looks down at the jammed opening once more, the paper has been torn along its edge, she is puzzled, she would like to say

Unlock the door then pull the paper from the outside.

She does not, she feels the restraint of inexperienced years, she moves her head away, her eyes remain fixed upon him.

Breathing heavily he pushes his lower jaw outward and grasps the ink smudged headline **La situación es más grave que nunca**. *At last he jerks it loose, he sighs. Patting the paper with the back of his hand as if to an old friend he whispers into its pages*

Free from the clutches of the outside world.

He looks up.

Rosa?.. I'm glad you're here.

He hurriedly searches for a paragraph entitled **A Journal of Indigenous Design**. *He cannot find it, he slaps each page noisily against the other, backs up two pages, scans the left hand page then....*

Here, Rosa, take this, you see? this paragraph.

He roughly tears the passage out and throws the remaining bulk sightlessly to the ground.

Cut this out carefully for me.

Rosa smiles and takes the piece of paper into her room where she places it on the table. From a drawer she finds a small pair of scissors, picks up the paper and begins to cut, turning the paper a full ninety degrees at each corner. She lays the printed column out in front of her:

A Journal of Indigenous Design

It appears our newly appointed minister for the arts, Signor Roul Lopez, has moved mountains in ensuring Governmental assistance towards the financing of a new quarterly examining our cultural heritage.

Signor Lopez has fought off the usual stampede for cash from the military and has held his ground, convincing other departments of the merit of this particular project. We must all applaud him in this cause. The journal will feature articles by internationally renowned experts in the fields of architecture, painting, sculpture, textile and ceramics. It is hoped that artists, craftsmen and dealers throughout the country will participate by submitting works that will be profiled, and that through publication a greater appreciation and pride in our national identity will result, both here and abroad.

Submissions to be sent to:

Signor Roul Lopez,
Minister of Arts and Culture,
Central Committee,
Government House.

Rosa feels the comforting weight of her father's hand rest on her shoulder, his bristled cheek now close to hers. They look on as if at a fragment of gold leaf, their breath shallow. He places his third and fourth finger under the final few syllables as she reads aloud the address of Signor Roul Lopez.

Minister of Arts and Culture,
Central Committee,
Government House.

A chance like this comes only once in a life, we have more than enough good work on our shelves to impress them. We could make a name for ourselves, branch out, in a year from now, who knows? A second shop? It will be hard, I'll need you at my side, you and I, we could do it, What do you say?

•

José has now completed drawing the arch of the church doorway and is beginning work on the old well which sits in the small square in front of the church, a large hinged wooden lid covers its mouth. He is lost in complete concentration as Father Luis Martinez passes by unnoticed.

The baked brick floor remains warm as you lay still under the diamond-centred blanket. It is thirty minutes since your sister left for the church. Your eyes open, you hear the careful crunch of sole to gravel. Father Martinez leans over a line of terracotta pots full with flowering desert plants and taps on the closed shutters;

Leticia, it concerns Guillermo.

The priest assumes a position of slight discomfort within the unfamiliar confines of her home.

The bus will arrive before daybreak.

So, you come about Guillermo. You are young for a priest, they say you have rejected a life in the seminary to be with us.

To live amongst your intrigue.

Our intrigue. . . you believe Felipe wants to harm Guillermo?

I am unsure.

But Aura, Aura believes so.

She brought evidence.

The necklace? Tell me Father, have you been in love?

Luis confirms suspicion through the silence that passes as memory. To such a silence Leticia entrusts the continuing life of Rosa:

As a woman who passed mid-way through her thirties, Rosa kept precious an air of youth, not of superficial beauty bought by cosmetic disguise, but of a certain quality of life like light behind her eyes. Women in the town had grown jealous of this and began to encourage distrust between themselves.

Under breath they would say

She wears a scent.

Yes?

A scent that in the folding of the cloth she leaves for our men to embrace.

And

She sings songs unseemly for a woman of her age.

And

Her father keeps a hold on her.

A church-going man.

An honest man.

All by the onset of occasion has become as grey.

Rosa's hair, which remained uncut since that scene of gathering flowers, touches the side of her waist as she turns to see who enters under the quickening to and fro of the bell's fading.

●

His clothes are of a softly settled fawn coloured cotton and lie loosely over his dark-skinned well proportioned body. His trousers are faintly creased, his footwear comfortably cool.

My name is Gabriel Diez.

He has cleaned and cut his finger nails. They remain unseen as he loosens his grasp on the handle of his worn suitcase so as not to appear desperate.

A moment of absurd hope

As on that evening when Rosa will open her father's steel strongbox without his knowing:

Inside the box you find a camera your father bought on his travels abroad many years before, it is unused. Beside the camera, with the words **exceptionally sensitive film** *printed in bold red letters, is a small blue-green cardboard carton. You take these to a place you meet with Gabriel.*

Within the wing beat of a hummingbird

Light enters the darkened space,

The camera's body charged with image:

Seated on a simply crafted stool by the open door of a large barn is Gabriel, he has a wide, relaxed and happy smile. Inside the barn, by the side of a bed of hay, dancing has scored the powdered earth. Love fills their heart.

●

Calmly;

Luis...

You feel these words fall like the gentle push of one domino to the next.

Father Luis... you come about Guillermo.

... But Aura, the necklace, I am unsure who speaks the...

No matter, remember, to live amongst our intrigue.

The disappearance of my predecessor, Antonio, I have felt ill at ease to mention anything of him until this moment.

Leticia wraps a shawl around her shoulders then turns to the door.

Come, you may ask him yourself, his was the murmur that woke José.

3. THE BLAZE OF HEADLIGHT, THE CLOSING SPACE

• • •

Foot flush to the deck you tap the glass casing of the temperature gauge, No change... damn.

You feel the uneven bite of brake chatter your bones.

Tendons strain, chins jolt firm against the chest, lips are wiped wet from dry as the rumble of the engine coughs to silence. The sombre lighting of the bus interior flickers a last pulse of life, the thin tone of wireless fades;

Ha habido un accidente. Esta a unos cuatro kilómetros de . . .

Guillermo rises from his seat and announces to the darkened cabin

It's overheated, nothing I can do, nothing any of us can do except wait. If you want to stretch your legs, rest beneath the stars, take a leak, go ahead.

He sits down again and opens a side window above the driver's door. Thought merges with the scent of his favourite tinned tobacco and the relief of stretching his cramped, now tingling legs.

•

You fold, your eyes unsighted by the darkness you unfold. Startled, you look up;

The young man with powder blue eyes nudges the fat man by his side, he is determined to wake him, he is polite but insistent. The fat man draws a deep breath from within his quietened world of unmoving, sighs then murmurs

Close to the fibre's edge.

To the fibre's?

The fat man lifts an eyelid and begins to talk excitedly. To the young man's surprise his voice is both sensitive and urbane.

It has been too long, forgive me, I play these games of pretending. You are travelling the country are you not? The clothes you wear, the books you read, the heat you feel. You and I, we have much to talk of, you wouldn't mind would you? Sharing small somethings of our lives before we go our separate ways?

Shuffling his unattended body he straightens himself up.

We'll make a deal, I'll let you out, then we'll talk, agreed?

•

The seats both behind and in front are occupied. You cannot cross the centre aisle and speak with her without collaboration. The old man who is younger than a first impression might imply, the fat man, widens his eyes offering a hand. You feel his steady grip, your neighbour's inconspicuous strength, you ponder on uncommon invitation.

Agreed.

The seat-back in front has suffered the wear and tear of seats too closely assigned. Knees have worn the centre cloth close to the wood, a plastic disc, hurriedly embossed, rattles against a nail driven untidily through its middle, cigarette burns have blistered the blackened foam-cladding that belches out behind the head rest. You stand precarious, unable to straighten either the upper or lower half of your body. Shifting weight as you stretch over the suitcase that lays as an immovable mass beneath you, you pass powder-blue eyes across the aisle onto the now vacant seat. Barely raising recognition;

You snag the pocket of your jacket on the numbered nail, your breath quickening.

The tick of metal,

Cooling to silence.

The old man continues to convince himself that he is entirely vigilant in his waking. More often than not the sounds of transit sedate him with repetition.

Cooling to . . .

Half-awake he whispers

Mind yourself. . . sadness bathes her beauty . . .

tick . . .

Silence.

Stale air scatters as you jostle with the concertinered door, a last shove and it lurches shut. Loose change falls from your pocket onto a mound of dirt pushed up by the sudden halt of tyres. As you move to pick up the spilt coins a worn piece of paper flutters end over end. You reach down, collect its fractured contents then look up.

Heat spills from the engine casing rippling the scene beyond;

Remote against horizon, her shoulder covered by her hand, the other tight around her waist, the vast dome of shimmering stars above, you stand then walk the fifty yards towards her. Muffled sounds from the bus interior dissolve with distance, soon nothing but the land, your breath and her silent image remain. Your voice alights beside her;

I found this, blown beside. . .

Thank you.

She continues to focus on a point slowly moving far away;

You have read it?

...No.

She smiles.

You should, read it now.

You read.

...An old friend.

Antonio?

Yes.

And the drawing?

My father's.

...You mind me asking?

She gently lifts her head as the point she has been looking at disappears across the skyline;

No...not at all...you know Gabriel then?

Gabriel?

The old man beside you, I saw you talking.

Oh, yes. we have an agreement.

To talk.

...Yes.

Good.

She loosens the knapsack which lays relaxed by her feet.

Here.

A small bottle of ink, a fountain pen, a sheet of paper.

You write well?

...Yes.

I need another's hand, a stranger's hand. It will not take long.

Pausing at the centre of each phrase for lack of light she begins.

Ink strikes the page;

Antonio,

I met Emilia in the recent past, she has brought much-needed mystery to my life. Do not despair, the loneliness you speak of is soon to fade from view. She returns to her home so we may marry.

Then your name.

My name?

Yes. . . your name.

. . . Francis

You lift the narrow bar that lays two-thirds along its barrel. Blue-black ink seeps into the valleys of your fingerprint as you watch her read the thin line that separates sand and sky. She folds the sheet of paper and places it between the pages of a small cloth-bound book.

Francis, keep the pen.

Then to herself;

A gift from Antonio. . .

. . . You have it now, I shall keep the book, he will understand.

•

Whispers of air pass the window, your cigarette burns unchecked. A voice from behind;

Hey, we get a move on?

. . . Lost them, you see them?

Eh?

Guillermo continues searching.

Look friend, the needle's on its way down. . . .

You raise a hand.

. . . five minutes.

In your distraction the small troop of ants that have occupied your complete attention advance single-file through a slender opening between the windscreen and dashboard.

Shaking your head, irritability

. . . Gone.

You place a thumb on the cold metal of the ignition switch, push down, then feel the subtle thud of electrical contact travel the short length of bone and cartilage towards your wrist. Knocking a knuckle against the glass gauge you hear the sizzle of loose wires, the struggle of a moth's wing. Again you tap the glass, a little harder, the hesitant spluttering of tungsten changes to a constant glow.

•

Francis, we should get back. . . .

The engine shudders into action belching soot and smoke into the frail night air.

It has been too long, forgive me.

Then holding the book close to your chest.

You will talk with him? With Gabriel?

A sudden shriek of air pressure as the brakes release their stubborn grasp. Hurriedly they return to the bus, their heads full with voice, the door clattering closed behind them.

●

Gabriel:

Limbs heavy as lumber at low tide.

The cushion to your left sinks.

The numbered nail sways.

The clutter of memory stirs;

... Powder blue?

Yes.

We agreed...

... To talk ... Emilia.

Yes.

You make the slightest gesture.

You want this?

For conversation...

He lifts the suitcase.

You snap the catch.

... small somethings of our lives.

You carefully unfurl the fragment of white lace which you have removed from the case, its delicately drawn thread-work carries an image kept hidden since the hour your only love left. In the softest of voices you begin telling Francis of that time, when a blast from the rear of the bus followed by a splash of glass on the roadside interrupts you.

●

Gabriel feels only the faint ripple of adrenaline pass along a vein which runs through the underside of his right arm, by the time it reaches his palm the sensation has all but disappeared. For Francis the sudden shattering of the brake light bulb arrives at a moment of intense anticipation:

It is uncertain whether the acute cramp that has taken hold of both your legs will subside as you try desperately to loosen your straining muscles. Ears prick as you let out a second yell of pain.

Here, take this.

Emilia passes you a glass, you clutch it awkwardly shaking a third of its contents over your shirt.

What is it?

Gabriel steadies your hand.

Go ahead.

You swill a mouthful back feeling the heat of hard liquor douse the tender wall of your throat, half gasping you hold the empty glass out in front of you. Gabriel wipes the rim dry.

You may find your legs numb for a while yet, the pain should pass soon.

Emilia's eyes graze the inner core of your pupil.

...Good?

The knotted sinews of your legs slacken.

•

Gabriel carefully unfurls the fragment of white lace which he has already once removed from his suitcase, its delicately drawn thread-work carries an image instant in translation;

As in that hour of leaving

You become

As hollow:

Rosa had spoken with you earlier that day.

She brought her closest memory, gave the piece of lace she peered through as a child and kissing you on the forehead as a mother might her son, she left. It was the last you saw of her.

●

Rosa, you must have kept the pain to yourself for some time now.

Your abdomen feels the searching discomfort of a midwife's hand.

It is your age, I am sorry. You will have the child?

Quickly you return to the store, your father is out, you look around, few things have changed. You grab a suitcase, fill it with some clothes, a towel, a photograph, then leave.

●

Disoriented by the constant shifting of the steering wheel a solitary ant scampers this way then that without any intention other than escape. Guillermo stabs at the wheel, wipes the tiny speck of blood along the outside seam of his trousers and returns his attention to the road;

The onset of inclination.

A mile on, descending, straining in fifth, revs retreat as you lift your foot and change into neutral. The blaze of headlight judders into the closing space between the bus and bed of the hill. You glance in your mirror. Alert, Gabriel sits very still, his face wet with tears. Francis watches as Emilia gently pats the old man's moistened skin dry.

The blaze of headlight,

The closing space.

Between the bus and bed of hill you think of Aura fearful in your arms. You force the engine into fifth once more, she screams. Stones hurtle sideways pitting the cacti which stand mute along the roadside.

The soft thud of encounter extends.

You glance in your mirror, you make out nothing but the restless confusion of shuddering light, you hear her voice;

Guillermo.

4. THE FULL-THROATED SOUND OF IMPACT

• • •

Guts spilt wide across the highway, blood bathing his drunken limbs warm before the final chill of death, he felt nothing but the full-throated sound of impact.

Several prominent people had complained of an excessive level of noise that interrupted the ambience of their evening meals. Their influence had assured that freight which was to be delivered during the hours of darkness should be off-loaded, often unsupervised, outside the municipal border and collected early the following morning.

Guts spilt wide across the highway, Felipe thinks he has hit one of the sacks that are left scattered by the side of the road. He knows the car is badly damaged although in the darkness he fails to see the dried red streaks that run crystalline across the bonnet. He continues onward, all intent now focused on arriving at the scene of his entanglement.

Foot flush to the deck.

Asphalt extending as a taut black thread into the distance.

A cold sweat of anticipation,

As on the night you first discover Aura by Guillermo's side. You fill with the sporadic impulse of association:

Palms compressed against the soft brown leather of the steering-wheel, a tiny fleck of glass dislodges itself from the shattered windshield and bites into the surface of your whitened knuckle.

The windshield, broken, how?

You've seen Aura?

Earlier.

She is unhurt?

Leticia pushes a splint of wood firmly into the belly of the iron stove then half fills the kettle with water.

Aura is in safe hands, tell me, the windshield.

You watch as the glint of glass burrows further into the soft swollen tissue of your hand.

Some thugs outside the courthouse, reprisals, my work, you understand.

Leticia wraps a cloth around the handle of the kettle.

Coffee?

Your face pallid, you remain unsuspecting. You take the cup, dousing your tongue into the scalding stimulant then look across its rim towards the window. Between the broken ribs of the shutters you catch sight of José and Father Antonio in the midst of a frantic exchange;

Two fireflies in a sea of darkness.

You mention Rosa, her father, Gabriel. You finish your coffee then stand.

Stay longer.

Thank you, I should get back.

You kiss.

As you begin to make your way towards your house you pull a handkerchief from your pocket and wipe the cold sweat from your forehead, a ticket stub falls from its folds onto the loose dirt. A whisper;

He's gone.

Shadows ripple across the surface of your hand.

You remain silent, stock-still, close to the ground.

Drawing your finger slowly back along the length of the ticket you hear the soft graze of a bolt as it slides loose from its socket. A faint slice of light exhales from the rear of the house, the sound of crushed gravel, fading, into the distance.

You wait a moment longer, turn, then cautiously make your way along the stone wall to Leticia's back door where you find a pair of black working boots neatly placed to the side of a step.

Scuff marks scar their polished hide.

A lace has been broken then hurriedly re-knotted.

Dog shit stubbornly clings to the worn heel of the right boot, the edge of the step is covered with unsuccessful attempts at its removal.

You inhale the sickly smell once more as you place your open hand snug to the door then push. The door silently opens two feet then comes to a sudden halt. You do not enter. The room appears empty except for a row of cooking utensils which hang at eye level on the nearside wall. Aura's voice draws closer together with that of a man's you do not recognise. You quickly pull the door back until only a chink of light punctures the widening aperture of your eye. You watch the swirling images of colour which speed across the row of cold steel blades and bevelled edges, slow;

Tell your husband... tell Felipe.

No, I cannot... Hold me.

You sense their tenderness,

Your rivalry,

The softness of their touch,

The guilt of inadequacy,

Your blood infused with doubt.

You wish to undo discovery,

To turn,

To act,

To lessen your desire.

You do not remember when you left Leticia's house or the short journey from her home to yours, an involuntary movement of protection. For the past half hour you have sat facing a large square mirror which occupies much of the south wall of your living room. You watch as the figure opposite slowly drags his fingers back and forth across the finely ridged grain of the hardwood table that lays to the side of you. You inspect the impenetrable composure of his gaze, the impotence of control. You turn away.

A cream coloured silk blouse drapes over an old dining chair in the adjoining room, ruffled blankets spread relaxed across the mattress. The man you have been watching stands and looks at you once more, you lower your eyes, then walk towards a music box which rests unlatched beneath the foot of the bed. You hesitate, slide the inner shelf away from the body of the box and remove a pouch hugging the soft warmth of velvet between your fingers, its weight, perfect in your hand. Loosening the ribbon that runs through its hem you spill a necklace out onto the woollen blanket. Although you have read the inscriptions many times before you lean the bedside lamp against the headboard, undo the clasp and hold it to the light. Running round the tiny gold hoop in two concentric circles are the words **To Aura with love José**. *The clasp carries the name* **Emilia** *which glints under the glow of the lamp. You fasten it back onto the hoop and return the necklace to its pouch. You think of his words again;*

Tell your husband. . . tell Felipe.

You hear her voice;

Guillermo.

You place the pouch in your pocket then shut the door behind you.

Dried red streaks run crystalline across the bonnet as Felipe continues onward towards the scene of his entanglement.

5. HE IS STILL WARM, FEEL HIM

• • •

It is the same each night,

The muffled murmur of another's dream:

Hunched over the handlebars with effort, the perished sidewalls of Father Antonio's tyres spread thick across the ground, he raises his head. The narrow track continues up the steep slope a further hundred yards. On either side, scrubland reaches deep into the darkness.

Rosa hears the distant sound of the single geared cycle straining to the top of the ridge.

Half a mile.

You tap the upturned scent bottle, sprinkling a few drops of lavender fragrance onto the pillowcase. You watch the steady rise and fall of your son's breath, calm beneath the bedclothes. You touch the tip of your finger to your tongue then gently wipe the dried salt from the corner of his eye. You listen once again. The chain clatters heavily against its guard as Father Antonio leans full weight on the pedal. Soon he will pass the untidy heaps of limestone wall which lay collapsed beside the entrance to your estate. He will feel the small of his back smart as the rear wheel stumbles, then cough to release a husk of maize which flutters at the back of his throat.

You take the cushion, pressing it into the yawning pillowcase,

There is little time left,

You look upon him,

A moment more,

You place it over your son,

Your son's face,

You do not wake him.

•

You have her house in full sight now. Streaks of light struggle through the lead-latticed glass of an upstairs window then scatter in all directions; Incandescent needles piercing the night sky. Brakes bite hard into the rusted wheel rims, your cycle falls noisily to the ground.

…Rosa…

You rush to the door fumbling for the right key in the darkness.

Quickly… here.

Touching the lock with one hand you guide the other until you hear the low thump of the latch dislocate.

For a time you stand silent at her side hearing the slow tapping of a twig against the spokes of your bicycle.

The cotton sheet, translucent with each drop of dampened sadness.

The twig,

Alternates,

Caught between two rods a tone apart.

Soon,

The offshoot,

Comes

To…

Rest.

He is still warm, feel him Father.

Rosa lifts her son's hand towards you, the colour drains from his fingers, she rests them back onto the bedclothes.

You whisper.

Compassion prevails only whilst a selfless heart beats.

She does not hear. You continue. Softly. To yourself. To Rosa.

There is a woman in the town, you do not know her. She has a daughter Emilia whose father José arrived breathless at the Church to ask if I could watch over the woman whilst he fetched the doctor. He was frantic. No one else would help:

Go now, hurry.

You hear his young legs scuttle dust into the quickly disappearing twilight. Soon you stand outside his house. Leticia opens the door, she has seen you through the window.

Father, this way.

She takes your short-brimmed black hat.

It began yesterday, in the evening.

You enter the bedroom, there is no sound other than the strain of muscle, no breath, no cry. You unroll the narrow sash you have kept tight within your palm, kiss the gold embroidered cross at its centre and pass it over your head.

In Nomine Patris, et Filii, et Spiritus Sancti.

Rosa watches you immersed within remembering;

Ad Deum, qui lætífiicat juventú1tem meam.

The words are distant, uncomfortable, she does not recognise them. She places her palm across her son's face then draws it down.

His eyes are closed now.

You are brought abruptly from a world of prayer.

Father, you must do something, Father.

You feel the tug of Leticia's hand on your upper arm, quickly your eyes open. She turns to her sister.

José will be back soon, Father Antonio is here now, he will help.

You take the piece of soft linen that lays to the side of you, dip it in a bowl of cool water then gently dab the compress to Aura's forehead. No relief. You try again; douse the linen, squeeze then place it to her temple. Still no sign of comfort. You pass the bowl to Leticia, asking her to fetch some fresh water. She returns. Once more you wring the cloth.

As Aura clasps her fists the tiny body constrained within her struggles feet first for a foothold. You search your wrist blindly for your watch face.

We will wait for the doctor, it is best.

You leave the room and stand by the window which looks out onto the street.

He will arrive shortly. He will. Very shortly.

Twenty minutes pass, the doctor is not yet here. The towel lays sodden beneath your arms as you ease the baby downward. The cord is entangled awkwardly around his neck, you cannot loosen it as the added strain would stop the flow of blood to his twin.

The paralysis of uncertainty.

Go on.

Rosa gently touches your hand.

You must go on.

The salmon pink flush of the nape of his neck rests against your palm. With the gentle curve of his spine supported by your forearm you place him quietly by his mother's side.

I had the choice between the first born or the second. I killed the boy. I do not know why I chose the girl.

Emilia.

●

Father Antonio's eyes soften.
It is all I can share with you.
You look upon the body of your dead son.
The scent of lavender surrounds him.

6. THE SEVERED FINGER

• • •

Pulling the cover loose Antonio pinches his eyelids together, shading them from the lamplight:

You rub your hand roughly to your face then look towards the table where José is working.

The time?

. . . Two twenty.

You knead the back of your neck, yawn, then stand. Your bare feet feel the rush of blood against the cool stone floor. You are still unsteady as you approach the window. Resting your hand against the table you look across the street. Your sight blurred; two figures, a priest and a woman. José lifts his head.

As their outlines draw closer their shadows swell against the loosely woven whitewashed walls which spread behind them.

Leticia, Father Martinez.

•

A simple wooden frame raises the narrow mattress one foot off the floor, cramped between its legs boxes burst with the work of countless wakeful nights. Antonio takes a mug from a shelf in the corner then partly fills it with red wine from a bottle that has been resting on the table.

Father Martinez. . . here.

Your thumb catches on a chip in its handle.

I am glad we have a chance at last to meet, you are no doubt confused.

His deeply browned forehead has been creased through spending long hours under the burning sun, lines flare from the outer corners of his gaze, his closely cropped hair bleached white. There is a kindness to his face. He pulls a stool from beside the bed, pauses, then raps it gently with the underside of his fist. He nods.

Leticia, I take it he knows at least a little?

You sit down. The base of your mug meets the floor.

•

Though Father Antonio's voice is certain his eyes betray his sadness:

The sharp tone of ceramic fills the air as Rosa brushes past a short stack of plates in the kitchen.

Father, stay with him, I will be back as soon as I can.

She hurriedly shuts the door behind her.

You climb the stairs towards her son's room.

Limbs heavy as lumber at low tide,

He is quite still. You draw nearer, then, at last, his breath, broad and even. You have not seen a body more perfect in proportion, a face more noble in expression. He rests untroubled before you.

The room grows cold.

You move silently through the house so as not to wake him. You leave the outside door ajar and walk towards the outhouse where a shallow basket lays beside its entrance. Firewood is heaped untidily against a wall, the timber roughly split in two along its length with a single stroke. As you throw the pieces of wood into the basket a splinter drives itself deep into the tender tissue of your palm. Pain darts, your hand lurches free, you scan searching for the splinter.

A chair hurtles through the upstairs window where you last saw Rosa's son. In less than an instant your eyelids snap shut, your head trips forward, your shoulders rise, your torso buckles, the chair shatters to the ground. You gather your senses then look to the window where you see his struggling form. An anguished cry crowds the air.

Your heart pounding, you take the stairs two at a time.

You are in his room now. The mattress has been overturned, he is battering his arms brutally against the wooden bedposts, his head moving violently from side to side, breath bursts from his body. You are afraid. You step closer, you reach towards him, he does not see you, he grasps the nearest object then tightens his grip. It is as if a shard of steel is forced through your vein. You cry out, confused he loosens his hold, you pull your hand free. You cannot ease the blind panic that consumes him.

Rosa...

She returns to find her son still shaking from her absence.

... there was nothing I could do.

His swollen arms surround her, the two of them immersed within the other's comfort.

Later;

It is the same whenever I am any distance from him, even for an hour. I am old, when I die, what will become of him?

You have no answer.

The following month she placed a pillow to his face and killed him. Leticia came to tell me I would be forced to testify against her.

The distant sound of a car threads itself between the tender strains of Antonio's voice.

I could not, she has punishment enough. And so, I have found myself here, in hiding, thinking of her love. The nature of it.

Wine sways from side to side as Father Luis Martinez rubs his thumb once more across the handle of his mug. Softly;

The Church knows of this?

She cannot, She would be compelled to contact the authorities. It was not a confession I heard but a crime I witnessed. Leticia brought you here so I could meet with you, explain myself before I leave at first light, it is no longer safe to remain here.

The police, they are looking for you?

An engine dies,

You turn sharply to the window, a plume of dust rises, the sound of a car skids to a halt. The door opens, you wait for it to slam shut in the silence.

José looks out along the street.

It is Felipe.

Your heartbeat lessens. A single beam of light slants uncomfortably from the front of his car.

He's outside the church, seems to be in a hurry.

... I'd better go, I might be needed.

You shake Farther Martinez by the hand.

Sure, take care.

Don't worry, we'll sort this out somehow. . . .

He nods;

... Leticia, José.

•

You have always admired Felipe's cream Mercedes from afar, you stop yourself from calling out to him as he disappears around the side of the church, a thought distracts you;

Antonio leaving, first light.

You peer inside the car, you smell the dark blue leather upholstery, you inhale, deeply. A worn suitcase rests on the rear seat, the left lock open, the right shut tight, documents pushed out between its jaws like a half-eaten meal. The butt-end of an expensive cigarette smoulders in the ash tray. Your eyes trace the faint ripples of smoke upwards until, reaching the window wiper stain, they shift focus. Streaks of blood glint like powdered glass in the darkness.

The nearside headlamp has been wrenched from its socket, coloured wires hang like nerve ends, jumping as the copper tips touch the raw metal. Tiny spikes of light tingle against the crumpled chrome of the grill. Lodged between its blood-spattered teeth is the severed finger of a man. You place your thumb to its soft underside, it is still warm from the heat of the engine. Taking a handkerchief from your pocket you wrap it round the finger, then, delicately moving it from side to side, you ease it gently outwards. As you lightly squeeze the nail a small amount of blood flows through the joint one last time, the flexed knuckle straightens stiff.

The finger lays like a wrinkled prune within the soft folds of the milk-white cloth. Felipe has not seen you approach, his hand is blindly searching behind a stone slab which rests up against the church wall.

Can I help?

In one sudden startled movement he turns around.

Father Martinez. No... no thank you, I am fine.

It is late. What happened to the car?

I hit something outside the town, not sure what, I was in a rush, I...

He catches himself mid-sentence then returns his arm to the small space between the slab and wall.

You injured someone.

For a moment he hesitates then shakes his head.

Couldn't be. . .

He continues, preoccupied;

. . . would have known it.

Is it the necklace you are looking for?

He inspects your gaze.

You know? Show me.

It is somewhere safe. You say the accident took place outside. . . .

He raises his hand cutting you short.

I'll sort that out later, the necklace, where is it?

I found this, wedged in the grill of your car.

You show Felipe the contents of your handkerchief, the colour drains from his face.

But. . .

We must go back.

The engine roars, your focus anchored firm to the skyline.

How far?

Eight, ten minutes perhaps.

Wooden stakes line the side of the road in thousand yard intervals, nailed to their shafts are the weathered remains of a notice;

. . . That interrupts the quality of life in our town. Henceforth, freight which . . .

Red letters waft in the light fitful breeze;

No further correspondence shall be entered into.

As the cream Mercedes sprints past, the rush of wind tears one from its moorings.

•

Guts spilt wide across the highway, the shallow pulse of your vein fades. You have left a carpet of blood and booze on the rough tarmac where you have dragged yourself the fifty feet towards your house. You lack all sensation from your chest downwards. Reserve spent, you have only the final breath of thought before you die. It is of the soundless image of your dog's lifeless body lain on the thin slabs of fired clay which blanket the floor of a stranger's house:

Facing the splinters of wood which jut out from the doorframe where you forced your entry an hour ago, you sit waiting on a chair you have dragged from a neighbouring room and positioned a few feet from your dog's corpse. You brush a fleck of glass from the edge of the page you hold then check the top left hand corner of the roughly creased document;

Felipe Delgardo, Pueblo del Pocito.

You took the page from the open jaws of a worn suitcase resting on the rear seat of a cream Mercedes parked close to the side of the court house building. No one saw you walk down the twenty three steps which unfurl wide like a giant fan from its entrance. You loosened a small brass ring the size of your fist from the crumbling sandstone wall then threw it at the only car which stood nearby. Its windshield split instantly into a labyrinth of shattered glass. You tapped the lower portion of the window, a curtain of air fell from along its top edge, fragments spread as pale points of light on the powdery earth.

You look at your dog's broken frame once more as the door swings open. Aura faces you.

Who are...

Your name Delgardo?

She is as still as if a poisoned fang is set to strike. The rancid odour that trickles from the dog's flaccid body reaches her. The corner of her eye trembles as she fastens her sight firmly to the animal.

Go ahead, look . . . She'd be alive if those shit-heads left things as they were. It's my home not some municipal dumping ground.

You crumple the page in one sharp movement of your hand then let the paper drop to the floor.

I have sat waiting for you, your husband.

You slowly raise yourself from the chair then walk towards her until your bristled cheek rubs rough against her temple. You whisper.

You're all the same. Out of sight, out of. . .

Aura smells the drunken sweat of your breath:

Bury her.

Your eyes close.

●

The front suspension sinks as you pump the pedal twice and point.

There, you see him?

The car comes to a standstill, you turn the key, the engine quits. You trace the trail of blood back along the road, torn shreds of flesh snag the coarse gritty surface. Soon Felipe is crouched over the dead man's body, frantic in his desperate effort to reclaim him from the silence that enfolds him.

Felipe.

He does not hear.

Felipe, enough.

His arms locked at the elbows, he leans his weight full to the dead man's chest.

Damn you.

You place a hand to the dead man's forehead.

I, by the power of Almighty God and the authority of His Church, absolve you from all your sins, in the name of the Father, Son and Holy...

You lower your head.

... We'll have to let his family know. Do you recognise him?

Felipe aims his eyes to the only house that stands along the roadside.

Here, help me get him up.

•

Police?... I'm reporting a road accident... My car... Felipe Delgardo... That's right... West, just outside town... No?.. A man's been killed... wait, I think...

You search for something with his name on.

Georgio Sánchez... Yes... No relatives... Myself? For God's sake, look, I'll come down... but... A moment.

You hand the phone to the priest.

Father Luis Martinez speaking... Pueblo del... You do?... I'll hold.

You press your palm to the mouthpiece.

He's finding a file on the dead man.

The thin voice extends once more from the phone.

Yes?..

You look towards Felipe.

... No doubt... Yes, you are certain about this?..

You find a pencil.

Go ahead... Nine, one, two, five.

The line snaps shut.

●

You lay flat on your back, sound asleep, your bloated belly rumbles, distant thunder, the quilt has been pushed thoughtlessly with your feet to the end of the bed. The chandelier quivers in sympathy as your wife lets out a deep guttural snore, your mouths remain agape.

You are woken with the jabber of bells. Confused, your eyelids unpeel.

The phone.

You lift the receiver then instantly place it back down. The clamour choked, you sink back into sleep. A minute more. Again the phone rings. You lift your head, raise your arm then draw the earpiece near.

Yes, yes.

You swallow then clear your throat.

This better be important. . . Eh? . . Sánchez. . .

You grow alert.

. . . Yes.

You smile.

No, no need. . . Of course, an accident. . . pure formality, so far as I am concerned the matter is closed. . . No, not at all. . . Goodnight.

You reach over, drop the earpiece back into place then mumble

I'm glad, he was getting to be a pain in the arse.

You cuff the pillow then return to sleep.

●

You look at the dead man slumped across the floor, his middle finger missing.

We'll take him back.

With us?

Yes, you have charge of the coroner's duties tonight.

But. . .

You said yourself he has no family.

No. . .

The police aren't concerned, the magistrate accepts my assessment. Tell me, did you kill him intentionally?

No.

Well then.

Wait just. . .

Felipe, you believe in God, I am a priest, there is no need for further talk.

Why take him back to Pueblo del Pocito?

I'll need your help, his death need not be worthless, trust me.

7. THE HEAT OF SECRECY BURNS BETWEEN YOU

• • •

Guillermo steps out into the dry warmth of night, his attention is snatched by the tortured shriek of a clutch recoiling from a miscued gear stick. A blue pick-up truck darts from a side street:

Your lungs fill with diesel fumes, your eyes pursue the squally cloud of dirt into the distance until the wilderness that faces you swallows all trace of the truck's feverish course.

Still tasting the stale odour of half-ignited fuel, you follow the truck tracks back to within a few feet of Aura's door. Water seeps from underneath its frame, the light is on inside. There is no sign of Felipe's cream Mercedes, you tap twice.

Aura.

The slosh and slap of water.

She drags the bucket hastily across the floor, the door swings open.

Guillermo.

She hurries you inside.

What has...

I can't let him find this, he would not forgive himself.

With her back to you she scrubs fresh blood stains from the slabs of fired clay. Your arms wrap tight around her.

Wait.

Straining;

It is almost done.

The final streak of blood is wiped away.

Over there, help me.

Out of sight in the corner of a nearby room on a piece of thick black P.V.C. lays the dog's stiffening body. You take it to the scrubland that stretches out behind the house.

The spade sinks into the soft earth with a single stroke. Soon a small mound of dirt is all that remains.

I must see Leticia before Felipe returns.

She lightly touches your forearm.

Go back to the house and brush the tyre tracks from outside the door, I shall meet you at Leticia's.

Gently;

Thank you.

•

You unfold the diamond-centred blanket that has lain length-ways beside you. Your eyes remain open. A rap at the door, you are startled.

Aura.

I have little time, Felipe will be back soon, he will ask for me, tell him I am safe.

You are shaking.

The Burial of Georgio Sánchez

●

You have left your boots by the side of the back door step. As the hardened soles of your feet cross the cold tiled floor you hear Leticia's voice.

. . . It is better that he knows.

You break the silence.

That who knows?

An open-handed smack of adrenaline smarts her face.

Is that you? Guillermo?

Aura tells you Georgio Sánchez had broken-in through the front door then sat for an hour with his dog's blood-soaked carcass stretched out in front of him.

He'd been drinking.

If he so much as touched. . .

He blamed anyone connected with the courthouse for the dog's death, said none of them gave a damn about what happened outside the town. He was blind with. . . .

The passion of injustice eh? I'll find him. . .

You turn to the door.

. . . the man needs a lesson, he wont be back in a hurry.

Wait, what if you're seen and Felipe finds out? He'll finish with his work if he thinks I've been put at risk because of it.

You lift the latch.

It's too important to him.

You pause.

. . . He'd have nothing.

The unmistakable sound of Felipe's cream Mercedes draws into town. The latch drops back into place.

His windshield is shattered.

Leticia points to the next room.

The light.

You stand motionless beside Aura.

A rap at the door.

Felipe, come in.

The heat of secrecy burns between you.

You're cold, take this.

You've seen Aura?

Earlier.

She is unhurt?

Yes.

And Father?

He is with José.

Snatching short shallow breaths through a narrow crack that barely separates your lips, you hear Leticia in the next room push a splint of wood firmly into the belly of the iron stove then half fills the kettle with water.

Looks painful.

A splinter of glass, some thugs outside the courthouse smashed the windshield. It'll be alright.

Coffee? . . Trust me, Aura is safe.

Your eyes close.

You mentioned an old woman, you say...

For a time the sound of voices fade, you sense only the fragrance of apple as the loose knot of hair that Aura tied earlier slackens then falls softly against you.

Stay longer.

Thank you, I should get back.

A whisper:
He's gone.
…Rosa.
You heard? Father Antonio knew her, I should tell him.
Leticia, the back way.
The soft graze of bolt slides loose from its socket. She is gone.

…Listen to me, Sánchez won't come back, he'd had enough, that is all.
And what if someone else who's had enough finds where you live, I don't like it.
Guillermo it'll be alright.
You glance at the door.
Tell your husband…tell Felipe.
…I cannot…Hold me.

You sense her tenderness,
The softness of her touch,
The blaze of headlight,
The closing space,
The restless confusion of shuddering doubt,
Unsettled voices raised behind you,
An air horn lowering pitch,
Your torso tilts.

Gabriel turns as the lorry's load scrambles by;
Our driver's not for the faint hearted.

●

Francis does not hear him:

You slowly roll the barrel of the fountain pen between the fingers of your right hand.

The priest gave that to her before she left.

Antonio? He is a priest?

He knew her father, he's not been seen for some time, six, eight months, I lose track.

Gabriel looks at Emilia who is now facing the window.

The two of them were close.

You inspect the barrel of the pen once more then slip it into your jacket pocket.

I wrote a letter to him, back there where the bus stopped.

... She asked you to.

The green cloth-bound book rests beneath her hand. You trace the smooth contours that trail from the shadowed edge of her eye to the soft curve at the nape of her neck, her darkened skin glistening with a thin film of sweat. Your focus sharpens on the tiny movements at the corner of her lips, you place her voice;

Another's hand, a stranger's hand.

With attention firmly fastened to the skyline she feels your eyes upon her.

At the front of the bus a boy plays with a torch he has found tucked away behind the driver's seat. He slides his thumb across the shiny chrome switch then points it at the mirror high above him. Light darts dazzling the broad shouldered man whose hands clench the steering wheel. His foot stabs suddenly at the centre pedal. The torch tumbles to the ground as the boy's mother cuffs him hard around the ear.

Estúpido.

You do not notice the uneven growl of engine or that Gabriel rubs his forehead briskly with the heel of his hand.

Her lips are now quite still, without breath...

Powder blue, the letter, what does it say?

A little louder:

The letter.

A rose-red patch the size of a peach glows above his eyebrow, Gabriel smiles;

I understand, Emilia, as certain as a compass needle.

Placing a hand on your shoulder he leans across you.

Show him the book, go ahead, it is only fair.

You have crossed the centre aisle to speak with her. The warm haze of her breath spreads softly on the window pane. Her words taste delicate, tempered with sadness;

You wonder why I look towards the skyline, whether you might come to know me, what secrets I may hold, when we shall touch...

She hands you the book.

...Letters from my first love. I shall never be the same to you.

8. THE HALF-LIGHT

• • •

It is well over an hour since Father Luis left to speak with your sister. You have watched the church of San Juan Bautista darken as votive candles spill their last warm tears of wax onto the terracotta floor. The slow-paced hypnotic heartbeat of the church clock accompanies your whisper.

He should be here by now.

You have thought of the night Georgio Sánchez broke in through the door, and later, when Guillermo held you, the kindness of his touch. The thirst of concealment.

A shaft of light briefly catches the stained glass above the altar, car wheels stutter over the stony ground to the rear of the church. Your stomach sinks.

Felipe.

The sound of voices, the flick of a switch.

. . . Into the sacristy.

Shadows spread past the wooden pew where you sit. Straining, Father Luis and Felipe lift a man's body up onto the table, his arm swaying loosely from its shoulder.

You've got him now?

Yes, gently.

The table creaks beneath his weight.

Here, take this.

The priest passes a folded altar cloth from a closet behind him, shaking it loose Felipe lays it over the man then pauses.

. . . We must go.

You are about to come forward from the half-light to show yourself when Felipe puts an open hand to the priest's chest.

The necklace, you've not forgotten?

You do not move.

I was with Father Antonio earlier . . . The fewer involved in this the better.

You've seen him?

He's leaving at first light, the police, you understand. He's done nothing wrong Felipe . . . If he could have been involved in an accident, killed . . .

Felipe turns to the table.

The case against Rosa, he's the only witness, right? They would both be free.

You look on unseen.

Father Luis makes a motion towards the dead man.

We can't bring him back Felipe . . . Some good can come of this.

. . . If I do this, you'll give me the necklace?

You have my word.

They leave, the high pitched patter of keys tap against the outside of the door. You wait the half minute before your eyes grow used to the dark then slowly make your way over to the table where the man lies. Before you lift the cloth from his face you gently touch its lace edge with the tips of your fingers. You take a short breath, pull the cover loose then place the back of your hand close to his mouth.

It is difficult in the darkness to make out who the dead man is, you draw closer. A deep gash choked with congealed blood runs downward at an angle from the black hair of his left eyebrow to the base of where his jawbone meets his skull, his earlobe has been torn free.

Sánchez.

You carefully lower the altar cloth.

●

The shutters are closed, the door locked, the diamond-centred blanket wraps Leticia in a deep dreamless sleep:

You do not hear Felipe and Father Luis cross the atrium in front of the church and make their way to José's house.

●

It's alright, he's come to help.

You take a long look at him.

It's been a while . . . Felipe.

José.

. . . Come in.

Where's Leticia?

She left after the two of you drove off, what's happened?

It was an accident, his car.

I killed a man, didn't see him, Georgio Sánchez. We reported it but no one wants to know, he's in the church.

The police?

I spoke with the magistrate, he said Felipe should handle it.

Georgio.

Antonio's voice steps out from behind the wall of the neighbouring room.

You brought him back to the church?

Your eyes search the darkness.

Yes, Father Antonio, there's something else.

You offer your hand to the empty space.

You've come to make me testify.

No Father. Luis, tell him.

You said earlier, Rosa has suffered enough.

Muffled lamplight falls across the lower half of Father Antonio as he moves forward.

. . . Go on.

You cannot bear witness if you've been given a burial.

Closing his eyes the priest passes a hand over his closely cropped hair then kneads the bridge of his nose between his thumb and forefinger. To himself;

On the knife-edge of just deception.

José would have to sign his name to the formal identification.

You could never return.

Sánchez? . . take my place?

José turns to Luis then to you.

I can't believe. . .

They'll keep after Rosa, you know that, it's a way out.

Father?

. . .

You are willing to make the papers up?

You give a short nod.

Unfairly, it is up to José.

You have fetched your hide briefcase from the car, it lies on the desk. You pull a pen from a small partition which runs along one side, it is a pen you only use when concluding your duties as coroner.

You look at the blank certificate.

José is right to hesitate, if it wasn't for the necklace…

Before this last thought comes to rest you watch your hand enter the priest's name under deceased;

Antonio Sientos.

Sixty three.

Catholic priest.

Church of San Juan Bautista, Pueblo del Pocito.

None.

Traffic accident.

Approximately two twenty a.m.

Twelve miles due east on highway.

Unknown.

Multiple injuries.

No.

José looks across the desk to the drawing of the church, which he has all but completed. As he raises his head he catches sight of Aura quickly leaving the building.

José?

Felipe and the two priests have kept their eyes fixed upon him. He turns to them.

Show me.

Felipe points to the first of three lines at the lower right hand side of the paper. He takes the pen.

José Cabrera.

The others follow.

Luis Martinez.

Felipe Delgardo.

You remove the large elastic band which keeps the official stamp firmly to the ink pad then change two digits so that it reads today's date. In quick succession you strike the pad hard then the paper. You slip the document into an envelope addressed to **The Chief Registrar.**

Take this to the post-master as soon as he arrives, it must reach Government House by mid-day.

José rests the envelope on its edge on a high shelf in the bookcase.

It is best you leave within the hour, Father Luis and I must attend to Sánchez.

Felipe looks towards Father Antonio for a last time.

Thank you.

He nods.

Goodbye... Luis.

Father.

•

They are gone.

I should get my things together.

José glances across at the bookcase where a wicker basket, a quarter full with scrunched up paper, rests on the floor beside the lowest shelf.

It's not too late, I can still catch them.

Antonio has not heard, he has been thinking of his leaving, his emptiness, his loss. As he shakes himself loose from the conflict of his need he pulls a small pillbox from his pocket then places it gently in your palm.

When you next see Emilia give this to her, tell her I am sorry for not staying.

A few insufficient moments remain.

You wrap the other in your arms then pat him on the back.

There are no words.

Saw to the bone your limb falls free.

●

The coffin maker's house stands on its own at the end of a narrow street. A large black limousine is parked outside. As you pass the car the back of your hand runs along the smooth waxed paint work polished late last night.

He's going to think it strange.

Leave it to me.

A short man with bow legs, a large smile and a high voice comes to the door.

Felipe, it's early, what can I do for you?

There's been an accident, it's Father Antonio.

Surprised, he rubs one side of his coarse moustache.

Antonio . . . He's dead?

Yes.

Sorry to hear that. You want me to come over, I'll fetch my things.

Don't worry, the two of us can take care of this. If you could deliver the coffin, perhaps call by the church a couple of hours before Father Luis begins the mass, say, seven a.m.?

The two of you? I'm a little confused, I...

That's not enough time for you?

Yes but...

A pathologist is due to carry out some further tests, it will take a while.

●

I see, of course.

Thank you.

You're welcome.

Although you realise your smile is misplaced you feel to change expression would signal the start of another conversation. You lightly tap the roof of your limousine with your knuckle.

Time is short, I'll bring the car to the side of the church around seven.

Someone will be there.

Right, I'll see you then.

You return to your house.

●

Felipe and Father Luis walk back to the church troubled by the coffin maker's smile.

I never mentioned taking mass... What about Sánchez?

Second thoughts?

It's just that... mass.

If we're to make this work Father you'll have...

Yes, I know.

You're sure?

The priest finds the key from the bunch then opens the door.

. . . Come on.

Half an hour further still from life, Georgio's body is as cold as the early hour, the pale grey-blue of his skin, sapless, stiff beneath the altar cloth.

Stay here, I'll get the necklace.

Beside the carvings of animals and flowers which encircle the rim of the baptismal font are two large pottery vases, each resting on a wooden plinth. You remove one, place it on the floor then lift the hollow block beneath. You think of what you have said to Aura, you whisper

Guillermo.

You take the pouch then return the plinth and vase to the side of the font.

What will you do with the necklace?

It will keep him away from her, nothing more.

You rummage about in an old tin for the spare key to the church. It is not there. You must have loaned it out. You'll have to stay to make sure no one stumbles across the body. As Felipe moves to the door you ask

Guillermo. . . you know him?

We know each other well enough, we have the one desire between us.

Mike de Sousa

9. DESIRE AND DECEIT

• • •

Guillermo stoops to scratch the rash on his ankle made by the line of ants he last saw marching over the dashboard. He awkwardly peers across the steering wheel, red taillights dart in and out of sight as the postal van which harried him for the last three miles passes the bus on a blind bend. He dips the main beam.

Idiot.

The rattling of the seat-stays smothers the soft flutter of paper as Emilia gently fans the pages of the cloth-bound book. The sheet you signed your name to earlier falls loosely onto her lap. She makes a further fold then tucks the tongue cleanly away.

Not far. . . you better take this, give it to Leticia, she lives half way along the mainstreet on the left as you look towards the church, her windows are set lower than the rest. Tell her Antonio must have the note as soon as she can safely get it to him.

You hold out your hand to receive it.

Don't mention this to Gabriel, it is better that he does not know. I ask a lot of you Francis, it is important to me . . . When I find a man to be with, commit myself to. . . Father Antonio will take the marriage.

Then to herself;

He may stay for that.

That's it then.

You slam the hefty metal panel shut, hook the padlock through a slot, return it on itself then press it home. You look up, the pinpricks of light which come teeming over the roofs and walls of the town are swallowed, imperceptibly, moment by moment from the east. The deep blue of night recedes. As you reach for the handle on the door of your van you hear a voice from across the street.

Wait.

You turn to see a man running towards you waving a large brown envelope in the air.

Can you... Can you take this?

Out of breath eh? Lucky you caught me. **Chief Registrar**, must be important.

You throw the envelope onto the passenger seat.

Sure.

The man looks at you as if he is about to speak when the bus you overtook some miles back pulls up to within a few feet of the rear of your van. You raise your voice.

You want to say something?

No... it's alright.

Pulling the door closed you release the handbrake, turn the key then push the pedal smoothly to the floor. As the bus retreats within your mirror you catch sight of the driver, he makes a gesture in the air then mouths a few short sharp words in your direction. Your gold-capped tooth winks in the half-light as you chuckle to yourself.

...don't blame him.

You head off towards the skyline.

●

More often than not the sounds of transit sedate him.

Let him be.

The driver interrupts you as you are about to wake Gabriel.

He's doing no harm, he can stay in the bus until he's rested, the old man likes his sleep.

Emilia softly whispers

Come on.

She takes your hand and leads you into the open. The street stretches out in a straight line in front of you, past the town's limits, through scrub and brush, across the flatlands then on until the giant folds of a distant mountain shroud its progress. Closing her eyes she takes a breath

Home . . .

And then, surprised;

Papa.

They kiss.

It is good to see you.

Their warmth spreads.

You are well?

Yes, and you, how are you? you're up so early.

There are always. . .

. . . Things to do.

Her father smiles at you.

He's been kind. . . a friend, Francis. My father José.

A long trip?

Yes.

You feel at once at ease with him.

How is?. .

Emilia halts mid-sentence. José looks towards the others standing nearby then draws her close to his cheek.

I have something for you at the house, from Antonio.

He is still with you?

Go to Aura's for now, we'll talk later, it is for the best. . . trust me.

Francis.

I came down on the bus with Emilia, we've just arrived. She told me you could get this to Antonio.

Leticia takes the note.

You don't know? you wouldn't. Where is she?

Emilia?

It does not matter, she'll find out soon enough, you'd better come in.

Francis.

You're the first I've spoken to since. . .

She pauses.

. . . He came in his black limousine twenty minutes ago. He told me. He came to ask if he could use the flowers outside my house, he took them all, I wanted him to.

. . .

You don't understand, Antonio. . . Antonio has been killed, hit by a car.

. . .

Perhaps you could tell Emilia.

Yes.

The mass is at nine this morning.

Your steps are unhurried, there is no sign of the small crowd which gathered outside earlier. Apart from Gabriel who remains asleep in the bus you are the only soul in sight. You recall the directions Leticia gave to get to Aura's house. You slowly pass the loosely woven whitewashed walls, one by one, their flat roofs, their shuttered fronts. The taste of apprehension;

Emilia.

You gave it?

Yes...

Good. What's the matter?

She has not moved from your arms since hearing the news. The left side of her face rests against your shoulder, her eyes closed, the scent of her fevered body pressed soft against your own. Little by little she breathes, the shallow movement of her chest, the faint puff of air against your cheek. In mind all you have been is given, all you have, is offered, silently.

●

Guillermo stands leaning against an old acacia tree whose roots jut out through the asphalt at the edge of the town. He has seen Felipe's car parked outside the church. For a second time in ten minutes he presses his thumb up against the rim of the tin, frees the lid and shakes his head.

I've a mind to...

Pulling a leaf of cigarette paper from a small green packet he gently tweaks a wad of moist tobacco and pinches the strands out along its length. He replaces the lid, rolls the tobacco evenly until the chamfered corners of the paper disappear from view, then brings the gummed edge to his mouth and draws the cigarette across his tongue.

Why not?

He returns the tin to his pocket, spits a few loose fibres to his side, smoothes the smoke between his fingers then lights up:

You turn to set off when a woman's hand grabs your arm, your cigarette falls to the ground.

Christ.

You kick dirt over the puff of smouldering ash.

Aura.

I've been looking for you everywhere, I was going to tell Leticia when I heard your bus pull into town.

Tell her?

He must have heard about Georgio somehow.

Slow down.

Felipe's killed him.

What?

I was in the church when they brought Georgio's body into the sacristy, they didn't see me . . . Father Luis was with him.

An accident?

Listen to me, they're going to make out Antonio's dead.

They're still there?

No, Felipe's back at the house, the lights are on. I think Father Luis might be with him.

. . . Come on, we'll phone the police.

We can't do that. . . Felipe knows about us.

. . .

He's got the necklace, he's going to say you stole it, he wants you to stay away.

●

You have followed him from a safe distance, watched his every detail. You stand covered from head to foot in shadow, too far away to hear their words. It is the first time you have seen them together, under the old acacia tree. You love her. As they touch, your hand involuntarily moves towards a pocket where the subpoena for his arrest is kept.

She may never forgive you for this.

You cannot stop yourself.

They do not see you until a dry piece of wood snaps beneath your foot, you continue walking at the same unwavering pace towards them. Your eyes are locked with his, absorbed within the uncertainty of his gaze, neither of you shifting focus for an instant.

He is broad, their bodies suit one another well.

So, you are Guillermo.

You look to Aura.

My wife.

You engage his eyes once more.

You know? . . I have a simple choice for you. If you continue in this affair I will be forced to bring charges against you, that I will do today. The court will find you guilty, it is without question, the evidence I shall produce in support of my case will guarantee your conviction. If however you undertake not to see my wife from this moment onwards, no action shall be taken. The choice is yours.

It is said, you have him cornered, you wait for an answer. You taste her sadness, bathed in beauty, the love she has for you, it is what you have hoped for.

. . .

I was in the church Felipe . . . You killed him? Georgio?

You look to each of them,

You say nothing,

You walk away.

Are you in? José? Thank God. You were right, the envelope, we mustn't send it, give it to me.

10. WHEN ALONE TWO THINGS REMAIN

. . .

Warning. Rock fall. One mile.

Sunlight slides slowly down the sheer granite face, a thousand feet below the tiny truck winds along a slender ridge that connects one slope with the next.

My wife? sit her on a bike and it buckles beneath her, she is all backside my friend, she is my one heart's desire.

He laughs. The crates of used beer bottles splutter their needle-sharp gabble through the cabin wall, he raises his voice pointing his thumb to the rear.

If it wasn't for that she would have left me.

That sound?

A shallow momentum moves you forward from your seat as you approach the overhang which has collapsed a hundred yards ahead. Although some rocks and dirt have been cleared away, the road remains too narrow for the truck to pass through, the engine idles.

Glad I gave you a lift.

He jumps from his cabin onto the tarmac and passes along the side of the truck. Unstrapping a shovel he shouts back to you.

Your name?

Antonio.

Well Antonio, we'd better get to work.

Your shirts darken with sweat.

Our house is small, a thin wall between two rooms. We have four daughters and a son, you mind me talking?

No, I could do with the company.

You lever a rock to one side.

She's a shy woman, there's no privacy in a home like that, our bed became a place for sleep alone, you understand?

You smile.

Sure.

A little over a year ago I changed jobs, began driving this truck. The first week was hell, the sound of those bottles in there, you can't sleep for the ringing in your ears. So, one day coming back from work I stopped in town, bought some music, thought it might help me rest. Picked up some Mozart, cultured eh? Later when I got back I moved the record player into our room, let the needle drop and, that Mozart, he knows a thing or two, my wife has never been the same since.

He has a wide relaxed and happy smile.

You move the last of the rubble out of the way then walk back to the truck. As you pull yourself up into the cabin he unscrews a large steel flask, belches loudly, then pours some coffee into a cup.

Want some?

Thanks.

What's that then?

You take the cardboard cylinder that rests up against your coat, carefully slide the drawing out then show it to him. He takes a long hard look.

The church back there?

Yes, a friend gave it.

He pinches his eyelids close together to read the writing beneath;

When alone two things remain, oneself and the memory of another.

•

Emilia.

I need some time alone, I'll see you after mass, you'll be there?

Yes.

Francis lightly presses his hand against your upper arm then leaves.

You are full with thoughts of Antonio when you see your mother approach the house with the driver of the bus, they are hand in hand. You rush to the door, undo the latch, then return to sit on a chair behind the kitchen wall, barely out of sight. You hear Aura walk to within a few feet.

Father Luis?.. He must have gone.

Who's this?

She turns.

Emilia... it's an old picture. You had a long drive?

I thought of you.

They kiss.

You look back at them then close the door softly behind you.

Felipe. What are you waiting here for?

●

As the limousine gleams in the early morning light the coffin maker flattens his hair in the driver's mirror, takes a clothes brush from the glove compartment and gives a brisk sweep to each shoulder. Your knuckle knocks twice against the window.

Can I help?

His high pitched voice penetrates through the tinted glass.

Father Luis.

The coffin glides effortlessly over the steel rollers.

Watch it, it's heavy, the sacristy?

Georgio Sánchez remains covered with the altarcloth.

Beside the table, here.

... you want to lift him down?

No, wait. I'd prefer it if Felipe is present, I'm not certain how long he's going to be, he's got to clear a few things up.

The coffin maker looks across to the body.

If that's what you want.

He smiles.

The mass is as usual?

Yes, thank you.

He returns to his car, closes the tailgate, then drives off.

Four minutes pass. A young man with powder blue eyes approaches you.

I came on the bus, it's my first time in these parts, can you tell me when things start opening up around here? I could do with a drink.

You're out of luck, not until mid-morning. I've a glass inside the church though, just a moment.

A last drop of water slips down the clear crystal, Francis brings it to his mouth where it seeps into a dry crack in his lower lip.

Thanks.

You're welcome. You're travelling around then?

I'd like to stay longer in one place, money only lasts so long.

. . . Could I beg a favour? There's a mass in the morning, a funeral mass. I hoped someone would be here by now. Seems like a strange thing to ask but, time is getting on. Would you help me move the body?

•

As you help lower Antonio into the coffin the altar cloth catches on a splinter of wood.

He is younger than you imagined.

•

The sun slowly climbs above the rooftops, word spreads.

Your house is empty, Aura and Guillermo have left together, your movements are deliberate, controlled.

I should go, I killed a man.

Your hand dips inside the pockets of your Sunday best pulling out a small crop of snow white mothballs. The mothballs roll from your palm into a delicate green glass bowl which is neatly placed on a walnut ledge to the side of the wardrobe.

They will be there, at the church.

You unhook the hanger then remove the suit and place it carefully on the ruffled sheets. As you move to the door you lightly stub your foot on the side of a music box. You bend down, pick it up, twist the key then leave it playing beside your creaseless clothes.

The brass bathroom taps sweat with condensation. You shave, pull the plug then dry yourself with a large towel. After you have dressed you take your patent leather shoes from the bottom of the wardrobe and buff them evenly with a soft rag. A crumb of black wax settles on your cuff. You blow, then flick it with your finger scuffing the speck of polish with your nail.

Damn you.

You take the music box which lays beside you and hurl it at the wall. You watch as it turns clockwise through the air then splinters into a thousand tiny pieces. You briefly close your eyes.

You tie your shoelace, stand, then walk to the next room where you collect a recent photograph of Father Antonio. You cannot stop yourself from thinking of her.

●

Your flowers have been placed close to the entrance of the church where they surround two elegant ebony stands which shoulder the dead man's coffin. You have spoken to no one since Francis came to your house to give the note for Antonio. Your sister sits with Guillermo five rows in front, she feels him briefly touch her lightly with his gaze;

Ink to the quill, flight to the feather.

You whisper

Poor Felipe.

You check that no one has heard. You look across the aisle. José waits for the priest, he is tired, he turns to his watch. Five past nine.

Luis nervously wipes the beads of perspiration from his face.

You must . . . Are you ready?

Yes Father.

The altar boy tightens his hold around a tall wooden post which carries a silver cross at its peak.

•

Francis is the only one to notice Emilia slip in at the last moment, there is no time for her to join him. The priest walks to the altar, the church is full.

In Nomine...

She glances at the coffin, struggling to maintain the memory of his voice.

Think... outside your father's house;

I must go, it is Rosa, take care on your travels, with luck I shall see you return before the nights draw in.

You repeat the sentence silently, phrase by phrase, over, again, until the fragile comfort of recollection crumbles. You look to Francis. No one sees you leave.

Papa,

I am sorry. I miss you.

I cannot stay. Antonio. I know you will understand. Tell Francis not to follow me, I have left the cloth-bound book for him. The blue enamelled pill-box is in my knapsack.

With much love, Emilia.

•

Francis tilts his head towards the muraled canopy of the church interior. Slipping his hand into his jacket pocket he reaches for the fountain pen.

No trace, the other side? Nothing.

You look down and check again, your pocket has a small rip in one corner, your pulse surges. Trying not to attract attention to yourself you search for where it might have fallen. As the stranger in front of you shifts in his seat a photograph slips from his fingers onto the floor. You stretch across, pick it up and tap him on the shoulder. You read the date, the name **Father Antonio.** He is not the man you lowered into the coffin.

Yes? . . what is it?

I have to. . . where is she?

The woman to your side tells you to be quiet. Closing your palm around the photograph you stand then hurriedly shuffle your way past her.

The fountain pen.

You take a last look back.

As the priest prays aloud he watches you move along to the end of the pew and glance at the coffin, he kneels, words fade.

Shading your eyes from the strong light you run to the main street.

She couldn't be far.

You cast about for movement. Way-off in the distance, beside the silvery leaves of a sage bush, a lone rooster pecks at the dry earth.

Her father's, she could be at her father's.

You gather your thoughts.

Gabriel.

•

You're not mistaken?

I tell you the man I saw was younger, I have to find Emilia.

You step from the bus with your case, the concertinered door slides shut behind you.

The book you never read, it won't make a difference to the way you feel.

This way?

Francis turns back onto the main street towards the church.

Her father's house is over there.

He scuttles dust across the asphalt.

No one is in, an oil lamp hangs from the ceiling, a letter rests upside down on the table. After reading the message he looks up, by instinct settles on a direction, then takes off as if his life depends on it.

In this heat?

You smile.

Gabriel catches his breath and sets his suitcase down beside the old well that sits in the small square in front of the church:

As you wait for the mass to end you move your palm back and forth over the coarse grained timber that covers the body of the well. Gradually you become aware that a piece of soft fabric tickles the leading edge of your little finger. You pinch the patterned cloth then try pulling it through a thin crack close to a metal hinge which divides the wooden circle in two. It is caught fast from underneath.

Forget it.

The prickle of curiosity:

Cautiously you lift one half of the lid, carefully swing it in an arc, then let it down until it meets the other. Before you have a chance the cloth falls free fluttering end over end.

Lost it.

You look down into the well.

Wait.

You strain, you almost, see.

The cold dull-brown metal rungs are set into the stone a foot apart. You look up at the semi-circle of light ten feet above, below you make out the faint outline of a figure slouched against the dry walls of the well.

A little further.

A fractured rung beneath your foothold fails, you stumble.

Careful.

You focus all attention on descent.

At last.

You step onto the dried mud bed of the well. There is nothing you can do. She must have fallen . . . The scent of lavender surrounds you.

. . . Rosa.

The Burial of Georgio Sánchez

ABOUT THE AUTHOR

Mike de Sousa. Born: St. Michael's feast day, Basingstoke, England, 1961. Michael Peter Lawrence Paul de Sousa. Wife: life-long partner. Son: constant joy. Father: a story teller and drunk. Mother: a fighter. Both died in tragic circumstances. Baptised Roman Catholic. Now agnostic. Two sisters. Raised by two aunts. Author, artist, designer, photographer, composer, musician. Self published. Dyslexic. Likes heat. Dislikes cold. Loves movies. Hates opera. Spiritual home: The Americas. Ambition: to forge connections. Favorites: Marquez, Mozart; Keith Jarrett; Rembrandt; Turner; Frank Lloyd Wright; Szasz; Ansel Adams; Rodin; Walter Keeler; Rickie Lee Jones; flying; a dog named Sam, salmon mouse served with a starter of avocado, salad and prawns; Paris.

www.mikedesousa.com

The Burial of Georgio Sánchez

Published by EyeInvent Publishing

All Rights Reserved: Mike de Sousa © 2012